ME AND SHE: OUR SCATTERED DESTINY

FIND A WAY OR FADE AWAY

SURAJ BAVDANE

INTRODUCTION:-

Hello everyone. My name is Suraj and I'm the author of this book. First of all, thanks for buying this book. It means a lot to me. I watched anime, so I tried to write this book that way, so everyone will like it. If you like anime, manga, and light novels, then this is the book for you. I just have one request for you all. If you like this and the story within it, please recommend it to your friends and family. I really need your support, guys. I really hope everyone learns something from this book.

Thank you.

Gmail:-
Surajbavdane24@gmail.com

Contents

Prologue

STORY SYNOPSIS .

This story follows a boy named Hiro and his life. When he was little, he had a female best friend. Her name is Azuki, and she is Hiro's neighbor as well. So both of them used to spend all their time together. They used to enjoy their childhood together, but their joy didn't last long.. On that fateful day. Hiro and Azuki had an accident. As a result of that accident, Azuki lost her memories and Hiro is in a coma.

A few days later, Hiro regained consciousness, but when he found Azuki, she was not in the hospital, and no one told him. As a result, he blamed himself for what happened. His personality began to change. He started to feel guilty about the accident. He avoided talking to anyone. He began to hate himself.

That accident is becoming a nightmare for him. So one day, he swears he will find Azuki no matter what it takes or no matter how long it takes. As a child, he searches for azuki in his neighborhood. He also tried to find her when he was in middle school.

Now he is in high school, but his personality hasn't changed at all. All these years, he is only trying to find Azuki.

Now what will happen next and how will it change his life?

This may be the story of the boy named Hiro, but there are different stories lies in this story. Every character has their own stories and problems to deal with, but with help of helping each other they try to find themselves and chase to live a happy life.

CHAPTER ONE

SUFFERING.

CHAPTER 1

Ahh! What a nice evening. It really feels good.

Ohh, sorry, where should I start with? I guess I'll start by introducing myself first. My name is Hiro Satoru, age 17. I'm in high school. I hate myself for what I did. I despise every inch of me. It's because of me that someone got badly hurt. That person is very important to me, but the worst thing is that now I don't know anything about the who's most important to me. It's almost laughable. It's a grave sin that I committed.

There are a lot of things that I don't understand. Like, what is happiness? When someone is smiling, does it mean they are happy? So, is smiling happiness? Possibly not. Someone's smile may be fake. Maybe they are trying to act cheerful so they use can hide their true self or their problems. So what exactly is happiness? I don't know either. The only emotions I have felt for all these years are guiltiness, regret, and sadness. What does it mean to feel happiness? Because I am unable to feel happiness!

How can people be happy or keep smiling in this world where sadness is everywhere, where hatred is everywhere, where jealousy is everywhere, and where people are greedy everywhere? But The good thing is that there is also happiness, but I haven't felt any happiness for a long period of time. That's not the only thing. For a long time, I haven't smiled from the bottom of my heart.

The other thing that I can't understand is, what is life? Is this what we do day by day is this the life? I really don't think so. They say life is simply existing, but all these years I haven't felt any excitement at all. Also, why are we born as humans? Why not animals? What is the purpose behind this? I really want to find meaning in what my life means.

I wish I had friends so I could live normally, but I guess it's not possible for me. Forget I said anything. As time went on, I began to talk less and hate myself more. Guilt, remorse, grief, and pain kept growing in my chest. Because of the sin I committed

Tomorrow is my first day of high school. I am not excited about anything, though. I will be doing what I've been doing these past years. That means I'm going to find her no matter what! For now, I've got to enjoy today's weather. It really feels nice to sit at riverside to feel this weather. I wish I could have been sitting here with my friend, but I don't have any friends, so it's a pity.

Next day.

Wake up, Here. You are going to be late on your first day of high school.

I have already woke up, Mom.

I'm off, Mom.

Last night I really had a bad dream. Actually, it's a nightmare for me. It was a dream about the sin I committed, and because of it, I lost something precious. To know about my dream, you need to know about myself first. How was I when I was little?

When I was a little, I had friend. Her name is azuki. She was best friend of mine. She was neighbor of mine. We were always play together. We were spend most of our time together. I was a crybaby when I was a little, but she was strong. She always support me. She always kind to me.

Whenever someone tried to bully me she always stood strong in front of me. She always protected me. We are even in same elementary school & also in same class. There are also lots of friends I had in elementary school. We always meet at park at evening for playing.

One day, I told Azuki that we were going to the park, but we were going by bicycle. We took our cycles and headed towards the park. When we reached our friends were already there, and they were playing without us. Azuki chastised them because they were playing without us. After that, we played for a while at the park, and then we headed to the lake. That day was fun. I didn't forget that day. There are two memories I have of that day. The first one is about what we did that day. It's a good memory. The second one is a fateful memory that I couldn't forget until now. It's a memory that became a nightmare for me.

On that day, a fateful incident happened with us on our way back home. After a while playing at river side, after some time everyone started to going home, so azuki & I also took our cycle & headed home. On our way back home a accident happened with us. After the accident, only a few seconds after the accident, I fell unconscious.

I really don't know exactly what happened. When I woke up I saw I was in hospital & my mother was sitting beside me. She looked exhausted. At that moment I didn't understand what happened to me. My mother also woke up. Her eyes were all red. It looked like she couldn't sleep for days. When she saw me she hugged me & started crying.

When she hugged me, I asked mother where is azuki?, but she didn't response. After that doctor came & checked me. Few minutes later mother came & I asked her what had happened. She told me about the accident, & that I was in coma for 30 days. I asked my mother again about azuki, but she didn't told me anything. I thought she might be resting in her house....

....Still, I know mother knows something about Azuki, but I couldn't understand the situation at the time. I can remember whenever I asked my mother about Azuki, her expression changed for a moment. At that moment, I wanted to see Azuki because it was my fault that she got hurt. My chest was getting heavier every time I thought about her. Two days have passed, but Azuki didn't come. The next day, they discharged me. At that moment, I was just thinking about seeing Azuki, but when we reached our house, I saw Azuki's house was locked. At that moment, I had no idea what was going on. Azuki must be resting at her house. That's what I thought, but her house is locked. How is this possible? Moreover, why is her house locked? I asked my mother again, she didn't tell me. At that instant, I ran and tried to find Azuki. That day, I searched the whole town, but I couldn't find her. There was a lot more happening that day that my brain couldn't process. My thoughts and emotions were all mixed up.

A few days later, I calmed down, but as days passed, my guilt was growing as well. Because of me, she got hurt. It was my fault.

When I started going to middle high school, I started to see her. At first, I tried to find her in my school, but she was in my school. Every day after school, I tried to find her in different schools. Whenever I got free time, I tried to find her. Sometimes I've gone to the park or the library to find her. Slowly, I searched the whole town, but I always failed to find her. At that time, I also saved some money in case I had to travel to find her. Years have passed. I started as a second-year middle high school student. In my second year, I started to travel to some nearby towns, and I found Azuki. Whenever I failed to find her, I lost hope that I would be able to find her. Guilt, regret, sadness, agony, all these emotions started to grow in my chest. In my third year of middle high school, I started to travel to some towns that I had never been to before. I had a map, so with the help of the map, I was able to determine the town whenever I went to find her. In all these years, I have never been able to find her. At that moment, I felt like I was so pathetic. First, because of me, she got badly injured, and now I can't even find her after all these years. I'm so damn pathetic. At this rate, how can I possibly be able to meet her again?

This is why I hated myself. Now I am in high school. I hope I will find her this time. I can't wait to see her once. I'd be more than happy if I got a chance to meet her once again. This is the wish I've had ever since that accident.

Sometimes I wonder what our life would be like if that accident had never happened. Will we be friends now? Friends ....huh?

Ever since that accident happened to us, I have started to spend my time all alone. I was afraid to go outside. I didn't want to go outside. I stopped talking to people, no matter who they were. I was talking with my family. At that point, I don't want to make friends with anyone. There was only one thing I was thinking about all the time: how was I going to find Azuki? I want to find out so I can apologize to her for what happened that day, and also, after that accident, everyone knew that I was going to blame myself for what happened to Azuki, so everyone was telling me that it was not my fault, so don't blame yourself. But I knew from the beginning that it was my fault and mine alone. As time passed, I tried so many times to find Azuki, but I was unable to find her.

Every time everyone around me had friends, but I was the only one who had no friends. As time passed, I started to become lonely. So I don't have anyone to talk to. I have become a completely introverted person with no friends. I try not to interact with anyone.

I know what my problem is. I also know the solution, but what I don't know is where to look at it.

I really want to change myself, but I can't change myself. It's like, "you know you are going to die someday, but you don't want to die." I am also trapped in the same situation.

Is it possible for us to become friends. Can we become friends again if I get to meet her again? If it's not, then that's OK! Anyway, I consider myself very lucky that she was my friend.

This is my high school. I hope I'm able to find her.

When I enter school, everyone seems so happy. From this day on, everyone is going to enjoy their high school life and is looking forward to making new friends.

When I entered my classroom, something unexpected happened. The moment I entered the classroom, I saw Azuki in front of me. The moment my eyes were led to her, I knew she was Azuki. I rushed towards her and the moment I saw her, tears just came out of my eyes. At that moment, I was so happy that I can't even explain it. All these years, I tried to find her, but I never imagined that I would meet her in this way. I couldn't stop crying because all these years I wanted to meet her, so I could apologize to her for what happened that day. Because it was my fault that she got hurt.

Don't say that. It was not your fault back then. I can understand how you have been feeling, but don't push yourself too much. Everything will be alright.

Can we talk privately?

Yeah,

You said my name was Azuki, but I believe you mistook me for someone else. My name is Sakura.

Why are you doing this? Why are you pretending to be a Stranger?

What do you mean by that?

Your name is Azuki, and I know that.

I will tell you the whole truth. Like I said before, my name is not Azuki. My name is Sakura, and also, I'm not from here. We just moved here a while ago.

So why did you do that in the class?

Because if I said this in front of everyone, it would be bad for you and you wouldn't be able to make friends after that, so I did this.

Are you really saying the truth?

Yeah,

I'm sorry!

It's OK, but we can become friends if you want.

I didn't answer her and walked away. I've lost all my energy. I really didn't want to listen to anything. I felt like my destination was in front of me, but it was far away! I'm was going to the roof. I was also thinking about whether what she said was a lie or the truth, but it didn't feel like she was lying, and if she was the Azuki that I know, then she wouldn't have done something like that. I know it means she was saying the truth, but she is Azuki.

When I came to the roof, I was so confused that I didn't know what to do. I lost my temper. I started to say something like, "What was that? What the hell happened? How did that happen? When? Is it because of an accident..? Is this because of my fault? Of course this is my fault!" It's totally my fault that she lost her memories. I'm so pathetic! I'm the one to blame for this. I had to feel happy after seeing her safe after all these years, but why is my heart feeling even more pain than ever? Is it because she lost her memories? What I have done!

Hey, what happened to you? What are you saying and why are you crying? ' Suddenly, I heard someone's voice. He was a guy. He is probably the same age as me.

[When Kageyama looked into his eyes, Kageyama saw a lot of pain, more guilt and remorse. Kageyama knew what it felt like to have those emotions in your eyes because those eyes were reminding him of himself.]

I wanted to stay alone for a while, so that guy stayed on the other side of the corner on the roof. After a while, I calmed down. After that, everyone was going home. I also saw that Azuki was going home. At that moment, guilt, sorrow, remorse, and torment increased in my heart, and I asked myself a question, "Who is the one who is suffering the most, up until now?"

CHAPTER TWO

PAIN AND FRIENDSHIP.

CHAPTER 2

This is how my first day of high school ended. Although I didn't attend it. It was the most unexpected day.

I still can't process what happened today. My heart was filled with joy when I saw her in the classroom, and I was glad to hear her words. I was so happy that I got a chance to hear her words once again. I could not contain my tears at that moment. I felt like all the troubles were over now, so I thought that we could both become friends like we were when we were little. But when she said that what she said just a few moments ago was just a lie, then it really shattered my heart into a thousand pieces. It really made me to screamed with every inch of my energy. I was really scared to think about it. I lost my temper. My heart started pounding and I started saying something, to change myself..? How the hell am I going to change myself when she is in such a situation and I can do nothing for her? Are you kidding me? People protect their friends, and here I am, the one who caused trouble for his own friend. I really am so pathetic! At that moment, my emotions were mixed up.

I didn't know what I was doing.

After that, I came here to calm myself down. This is a place where I can calm myself down. I come here whenever I feel lost or frustrated. A few minutes later, I started to feel better, so I decided to go home. I reached home.

I'm home, mom.

A few minutes later, I ate my snacks and went to my room. No matter what, today's incident is one I can't forget. It comes to my mind from time to time. It felt like I was stuck in that moment.

Hiro, come down to eat your dinner.

I went and ate my dinner. While eating, that moment comes to mind once again. I started to replay that moment in my head unconscious. I was totally spaced out. It really scared me, so I didn't eat that much. I started to sleep, so that moment didn't come into my mind again.

A few hours later,

Azuki Don't leave me. Please stay here with me. What do I do if you leave me? What will happen to me if you leave me behind? Azuki Please?

(He is sleeping and babbles.)

I woke up and, after that, I ate my breakfast.

I'm off mother

Last night I had a dream about me and Azuki. It was more like a memory than a dream. In this dream, Azuki and I were playing all day together. I saw we were in the same elementary school. When we played games in her house, when she helped when I was crying, when we played at the riverside, I saw everything that we did in my dream, but all of a sudden she started to fade away & I was the only one who remained playing. It was not a dream, it was reality, the truth! This time I was not scared because I had already accepted the past, but what shivers me the most is when all of a sudden I am surrounded by darkness. I started walking in that darkness. Suddenly, a light came from nowhere & it made a path under my feet. I was walking on a light. Suddenly, I saw a person walking before me. She was female...

But what happened at the end of the dream really scared me! I woke up. I was trembling when I woke up. I felt like I was suffocating. Tears were coming from my eyes. I was crying. It was terrible. At the end of the dream, she was walking before me and I was walking behind her. The distance between us kept getting closer and closer. As I kept getting closer to her, she started to fade away. I was going to grab her hand, but suddenly, she turned around, and I saw her face, and she smiled at me. Before I was able to grab her hand, she fully disappeared. That person was Azuki. I don't know what that dream meant. I can only guess.

Does it mean that Azuki is going to leave me behind again? Why is that going to happen again? Can't things stay as they are now? I know that I am a terrible person, but I don't really want Azuki to leave me behind once again!

After all these years, I am able to see her once again. I am fine being a stranger to her; at least I can see her. I am willing to carry my guilt to the end; it's just that I don't want to say goodbye to her.

As for now, I need to focus on school today. I need to calm down before I get to school. It'd be better if I didn't talk to Azuki for a few days. Although I have a lot to talk about with her, she's forgotten her memories, so it seems pointless. I think it will be better if I watch her to get to know her personality, so I will keep an eye on her for a few days. When I got into my classroom, I looked up at Azuki. She was talking to another girl. That quality of hers remains the same, making friends so quickly. That's good. Whenever I looked at Azuki smiling, I felt really happy after seeing her. Sometimes it's crushed my heart that she forgot her memories and it happened because of me!! All the painful memories of mine and her suffering come flooding back to me in an instant.

A few days have passed. I have been watching her the last few days. Her personality has changed a little bit, though she is kind even now. That's great. She talks with other people at ease. I don't know how she did it. Her personality is so nice. That's why I have admired her since I was little. I wish I could become like her one day.

Today, I decided to watch Azuki. I have been noticing that the guy has been keeping an eye on me since we met on the roof top. I wonder why? Watching Azuki today feels sad, because she is sad. I saw her that way and felt pain in my chest because I was the one who did this to her. If I hadn't forgotten her memories, I would've made her smile again. I hated watching her like that, but I couldn't do anything about it. I'm so damn pathetic. I came to the rooftop because I couldn't watch her like that. It was painful. What a pain!

In my opinion, pain is inescapable. Everyone in this world has to feel pain in their life. It's just a matter of time when you have to feel it. There is a saying that whenever you feel pain or frustration, just watch the clouds. It helps you feel relaxed. But even clouds have to feel pain. In the rainy season, clouds have to carry raindrops. And they also have to endure all the pain caused by lightning. After recess, I came to class, and I noticed that guy keeping an eye on me again.

After school ended, everyone started to go home. I was waiting for Azuki to go out of the classroom, but that guy was also there. When Azuki stepped out of the classroom. That guy came to the bench near my bench and said something unexpected.

It seems you have noticed that I am keeping an eye on you.

I wanted to ask you just one question.

Do you like Sakura (Azuki)?

You don't need to know.

I guess it's no then.

If it's great then, then I can become close friends with her. A very close friend.

(He tries to provoke me by making a situation like this. This is not that he wants to know, so he is saying something that attacks directly on my emotions, so he will get the answer he wants. He is expecting me to reveal the truth. I know this guy is good because he was the one who helped me that day. I guess he knows that there is something between me and Azuki. That's why he's doing this. But sorry man, I don't wish anyone to know about me.

Would you like to? I really don't care.

Oh, I guess you're a tough one. Sorry for that.

My name is Kageyama.

I don't know yours, but I will know it in the future.

Let's become friends. What do you think?

CHAPTER THREE

WHY I'M SO DIFFERENT!!

CHAPTER 4

Good morning, mother.

Good morning, Hiro.

I ate my breakfast and started to go to school.

I'm off, mom.

Yesterday, that guy asked me to become friends with him, but I turned him down. I can't become friends with someone because I haven't atoned for the sin I committed. First I have to atone for the sin that I committed. Then I will think about making friends. I hope I didn't regret it because of the decision I made yesterday.

Because the weather was so nice today, I left the house early. I have to enjoy this nice weather, so I went to my spot where I can feel calm. I feel bad for that guy. I hope he didn't lose his confidence because of me. Anyway, it's time to go to school.

Hey, there you are. I thought you might be already at school. I'm glad I met you here. Okay then, let's go to school together.

Huh..? Hey, hey wait, what are you talking about? We are not friends, so why are you saying something like that?

That's true, so what am I doing here? Well, I don't know.

What do you mean by that?

I already told you I don't know.

Why is this jerk pissing me off this early in the morning?

Hey, yesterday, you asked me to become your friend, but I turned you down. I didn't have time to play around with friends. I don't get it. I am not your friend. So why are you here?

It's true that yesterday you turned me down, and you're right, you said we couldn't become friends either. We are not friends, at least not yet, but we can become friends in the future. You never know what will happen in the future.

[It startled me for a few seconds.]

I am telling you we can't become friends.

[I never would've thought that he talked to me again after that.]

Yeah, yeah, I hear you. Now let's hurry or we will be late for school.

What a drag is this? I guess I have to let him do what he wants to do. I'll let him tag along even though I don't consider him a friend.

[But he came to talk to me so quickly after what happened yesterday.]

Is he an idiot or something? I guess he is.

[However, it made them happy.]

We arrived at the school. Jeez, coming to school with someone is seriously embarrassing. All of a sudden, people started staring at me. I'm not a celebrity or anything. I'm not popular either. I'm just a normal guy who minds his own business. So why were they staring at me? Why is that? I don't get it.

They started saying something like, “Why are they coming together? Are those two friends or something? “

We are friends, and also, it’s none of your business, so shut up. Don’t spout nonsense.

I don’t like it when people start to look at me. It creeps me out. Whenever someone tries to stare at me, it feels weird, and somehow I know when someone is staring at me.

We entered the school. Since we came early, there were some boys standing in the hallways. They also started to stare at me. Again, what was happening today? Wait a minute. It started to make sense to me. Something is different today. I’m not alone today. This guy was with me the whole time, and he was talking to me like we were friends or something. Now I get why they were staring at me. I guess now everyone knows that I’m a loner. That’s why they were staring at me.

A few days ago, I helped a girl without knowing anything. On that Sunday, I was going to my place where I often go. If I remember correctly, she was searching for her cat and that cat came to me. I picked up that cat and started walking. After a few minutes, she saw that the cat was in my hands, so she came to me to take her back. “Thank you very much for finding my cat,” she said to me.

The next day at school, when I was going to the rooftop, she came to me and told me her name and said, “Let’s become friends.” But as you know, I also turned her down. I don’t even know what she looks like. There were lots of people there at that time.

I kind of felt bad for her though. So I guess someone has spread a rumor about me ‘that I turned down a cute girl or I’m a loner or something like that.’ Rumors spread so fast. It’s so scary.

We entered our classroom. Again, people started staring at me. It really started to piss me off. It kind of looked like they were surprised or something. Just look away from me, but don't worry, it's not what you think it is. So stop staring at me. I hope this will end quickly.

I was at recces when I looked at Azuki. That guy was talking to her. How can he talk to her so quickly? The way they were talking, it kind of looked like they already knew each other, but I don't think they knew each other. So how can he talk to new people? Is this his skill or something? If only I had that kind of skill, I would've started living normally like everyone else. I'm so different from him! Nah, it's no biggie. Staying alone is peace itself, I think.

A few minutes later, that guy came up to me and said, "Let's eat lunch together; after all, we're friends now."

No, we're not. I prefer to eat alone.

[This basterd came here to disturb my peace.]

Don't say that. We're fri...

No, we're not.

Anyway, let's eat. I'm starving.

Is this guy deaf or is he just ignoring me on purpose?

What did you bring today?

Quiet. Eat your lunch.

Everyone in my classroom started to stare at me again.

Could you guys just stop that already? It's creeping me out.

It's been a few days since that guy has stuck with me and declared that we're friends. Every morning, this guy stands in front of my house. "Since we're friends, we have to go to school together." He says this every day. It's so embarrassing. But the good thing is that now no one is staring at me. That's good. Now I can live at ease.

In these past few days, I have noticed that this guy is really good. His nature is pretty good, and he is pretty good at talking to new people. This guy is pretty smart. Two days ago, he was helping some girl with a math problem or whatever. I have observed this guy. He doesn't say no whenever someone asks him to help them out and afterwards talks to them like they already knew each other. What a smooth talker, huh?

Also, I have been noticing for a few days that a guy from my class was staring at me whenever this guy stuck with me. It felt like déjà vu to me. Don't tell me this guy is going to ask to become friends. No, please don't ask. I can't even handle this bastard. I can't handle another guy. It will break my peace.

For the past few days, I have been feeling lively. It's been happening since that guy started to stick with me. It feels good, but sometimes that just pisses me off.

Next day,

Good morning, mother.

Good morning.

I ate my breakfast and started to go to school.

I'm off, mother.

Suddenly, it came to my mind. That guy must have been waiting for me to come out. When I went outside, no one was there. I felt relieved at that time. I can go to school alone now, but in a few minutes, that guy showed up, but the worst thing about that is that he was with a girl, and that girl was Azuki.

What's going on? Why is he with Azuki today?

[What is this guy's plotting?]

CHAPTER FOUR

KAGEYAMA'S PERSPECTIVE & HIRO'S DECISION!

CHAPTER 3

In this chapter, we are going to learn about Kageyama and what he thinks about Hiro. Let's get started.

Hello, my name is Kageyama. I'm 17 years old and in high school. This is my first time introducing myself, so I guess it was good.

When I was in middle school, I was different from the people around me. I often stayed alone. I was always looking for something. Maybe I was looking for some people, people with whom I would feel alive and happy. I don't have friends who people call best friends. So I wanted to be friends with people like that. I wanted to be friends with someone, someone like the people who are called best friends. Best friend who has always been by your side. Whether you're in trouble or not, they will be by your side.

It's not like I didn't have friends back in those days. I had friends, but I felt like they never considered me as a friend, so I always felt like I should not belong here.

Now I have started going to high school. Now my high school life has begun. On my way to school, I was thinking about how I should do things this time. How do I become friends with someone who will consider me his friend? Because I don't want to repeat my past again. I just want to live a happy and exciting life. I reached the school. Suddenly, I started to feel uneasy because I couldn't find the answer I was looking for a few moments ago and also, here there were people who were happy about their high school life. They are going to live their lives with new friends. It's not like that I'm not happy for them; I was happy for them. At the time, I felt like if I made friends with someone, I'd be able to live my life the way they Do!?

I went to the rooftop since I was feeling uneasy. I was sitting and thinking about my childhood. A few minutes later, something unexpected happened. A boy came onto the rooftop. He appears to be terrified of me. I didn't know what happened to him. He was really scared of something. He was trembling, and suddenly he started to say something like, "What was that?" What the hell happened? How did that happen? When?..

..I wanted him to calm down, but didn't know what to do. I had a cold drink in my bag, so I think it will help to calm down a bit. So I stood up. When I was standing up, I heard him say something like, "She lost her." It was something like that, and I ran to where my bag was. I grabbed the drink and ran straight towards him.

Hey, Hey, calm down. If you drink this, you will feel better.

I called him several times, but I think he didn't hear my voice. Finally, he looked up at me. When I saw his face, he was crying, so I asked him, "Hey, what happened to you?" "What are you saying and why are you crying?" But when I saw his eyes, it scared me. In those eyes of his, I saw pain, regret, guilt, and remorse, and it felt like he had been carrying this burden for years now. I know how it feels to carry those emotions, because those eyes of his remind me of myself. I was like this when I was little.

After that, I gave him some space so he could calm down. At that time, I was thinking about what would've happened to him. I have never met or seen such a person. He seemed like he had gone through tremendous emotional torture. I get scared whenever I think of it. I can't imagine how much the guy may have suffered. But I know that this guy has been suffering for years now. He has already suffered a lot, but he is still suffering. It's not easy to carry those emotions with you over the years.

It is a fact that some people forget their promises in a year or two, but he has been carrying those emotions for years now.

That!! Now I don't care if I get friends or not, I will help him. After that day, I started watching him. I wanted to know about him first. The only two expressions on his face were when I saw him. The first sorrow and the second happiness Sometimes he looks happy, and sometimes he looks overly sad. But whenever I saw him, the emotions in his eyes were the same as the ones I saw that day.

His mood was starting to change. I noticed something. Every time he looks at Sakura, that expression on his face changes. For that moment, he looked happy.

So I thought something happened between them or they knew each other. If they knew each other, what would have happened between them for him to look like that?

I continued to keep an eye on him. Many times, he noticed that I was keeping an eye on him. After a few days, I decided that I was going to talk to him and provoke him so I could get an answer. That way, I can know the truth about him. Today is the day I'll talk to him.I thought I'd have to say something bad about Sakura, so I'll get my answers by pointing out his weaknesses. But when I talked to him, I didn't say anything bad about Sakura. I asked him if he liked Sakura or not, because I wanted to become very close to her. It was all just to provoke him, though, and it didn't work on him. He said, "Do what you want; I don't care." I guess he was not an easy target, so I said let's become friends. Now let's see what he will answer.

Now we will see what Hiro's answer was to Kageyama's.

I was shocked for a few seconds. For the first time in all these years, someone asked me to be their friend. It felt good though. I think it would be good to become friends with someone like this guy. It would be nice. Because this guy is a good person, I'm afraid I won't be able to play buddy-buddy right now. I would have to refuse his offer.

Sorry,

I don't have time to play buddy-buddy with someone. I have some important matters to settle. There might be some other guys who want to play buddy-buddy with you, so you can play with them.

Oh, is that so? With the help of you, I might have gotten closer to Sakura, but now you have refused, so it can't happen.

With the help of me? I don't know what you are talking about.

Is it over or do you have anything to talk about? Because I have something important to do.

Yeah, yeah. I don't have anything to talk about now. Sorry,

I turned him down. It would've been good if I accepted his offer, but I can't do that. She is still suffering because of me, so I can't do this, at least not now.

Let's see what will happen tomorrow.

CHAPTER FIVE

THE SURPRISE.....!

CHAPTER 5

This is bad. Very bad. Is this guy for real? What did he bring Azuki today? What is he planning this time? What do I do now? What a calamity this is! Whenever he does something like this, it's surely going to be bad for me. Please God, please save me from this deviant.

Why is this guy doing this? What is he after? Look man, I'm sorry for everything, but don't end up in a situation like this.

Actually, I do want to talk to Azuki. For all this time, I have been wishing to talk to her, but I don't want to talk to her right now. I'm not courageous enough to be able to talk to her right now. I am not prepared yet. I'm so nervous. Now that I don't have a choice but to talk to her. I guess life is full of uncertainties.

Now what do I do? Okay, first of all, stay calm and think clearly. Now he is already with Azuki, so I don't have a choice but to talk to her no matter what.

Good morning, Hiro. Kageyama said.

Good morning, Hiro. Azuki said.

Goo.., good Good morning. Good morning.

Damn. I'm so freaking nervous. This is terrible. Damn. What should I say now? What should people say after "good morning"? This is more difficult than I thought. Consider this, Hiro. I can't even think of what to do. Damn, this is so freakingly difficult. How is this guy good at this? It must be because of the skill he has. Something feels weird.

Huh..? Why have my hands begun to tremble? Stop trembling, damn it. I think I am done for! OH! God, please save me.

When I looked at that jerk who plotted this, I saw that he was laughing at me after seeing me like this. This is happening because of you, you bastard. You are doing this on purpose, aren't you?

Did you complete your homework?

Y. Ye. Yes, yeah, sure.

Because of the nervousness, I answered three times that simple question. How can I be so freaking nervous right now? I have to stop being nervous.

She laughed at me after seeing how nervous I was. It must have made her laugh. Oh, how pitiful I am. I can't even talk to this girl even though she's been my best friend since childhood. I have to speak normally.

After that, I somehow started to talk to her normally. The nervousness I was feeling before has completely disappeared. Then I suddenly noticed that only two of us were here, so where did that jerk go to? He must have fled somewhere or must be hiding somewhere on purpose. I don't get it. What was that jerk thinking? He sure is a cunning person. Knowing his personality, he must have been watching us ever since he left us alone. Anyway, it didn't matter now, because we had already reached the school.

Both of us entered the classroom. I mean me and Azuki (sorry, I mean Sakura). It's an old habit to call her Azuki.) When we entered the classroom together, everyone started to stare at me. Damn this again. I had a nostalgic feeling about it somehow. Don't stare at me like that, you jerks. Now why are they staring at me? I didn't do anything; I just entered the classroom with...

...Wait a minute. I think I think I know the reason this time. Why are they staring at me? You are staring at me because I entered the classroom with Azuki. I mean, Sakura, right? I feel sorry for them now that I know why they were staring at me.I kind of smirked at them. At that moment, I really felt happy. I know what you morons are thinking. You idiots must be thinking about when the two of us became friends. But this time, what you guys are thinking is true! We're friends. We have been friends since childhood, but no one knows it except me.

I had the impression that this time her stare was more intense than the last. This time they were surprised but angry at me. Why are they furious at me? The way they stared at me, I was able to feel their rage, but why? Ohh, I get it now. I know boys must have a crush on Azuki, but why were girls also staring at me? Don't tell me, is she your role model or something? Looking at their reaction after seeing us together, that must be true. I think I'm dead now.

A few minutes later, that jerk showed up. He entered the classroom. When he entered, he saw everyone was staring at me, so he looked at me. That bastard just laughed at me.

Hey, hey, why are you coming this way? Don't come here. Please don't come here, you bastard. Look, man, something might happen if you come here, but he came straight to me. I was so angry at him because of the morning incident, so I grabbed his collar and shouted at him. You jerk, why do you...?

Then suddenly I started to feel dizzy. All of a sudden, I sensed that someone might be cursing me. Then I looked at what was happening in the classroom, and I saw some devilish faces staring at me.

That was a horrible experience for me. If you want to know what I saw, I'll tell you. So when I said it, all the girls shifted their gazes to me. I looked at Sakura, but she looked like she was lost somehow. But now I didn't do anything, so why are they staring at me? I felt like I was suffocating even though the window was still open. Are they staring at me because of this jerk? Can't you morons just see this jerk coming here on his own? ...

...Don't tell me that all girls have a crush on this jerk, but why this guy? Is it because he is a smooth talker? It must be it. If you have a crush on this guy, this jerk, seriously, when you have a handsome dude in your own classroom, your choice is just terrible. Don't worry, I'm not talking about myself. I'm talking about the guy who stares at me when this jerk sticks with me. He looks good though, but he is scary. Speaking of which, where is he? I looked around, so I could see him. When I saw that Bastard was also looking at me, I said, "What's the problem with you guys?"

So now our homeroom has started, so they've stopped staring at me. Thank goodness. But the homeroom class came up with a surprise. Sir informed us that we would be taking a small surprise test today, and that the test would be about math. The test is about the previous chapter that the teacher taught us, and the thing is, I don't think I'm good at math. I think I'm going to mess up on this test for sure! Not that I have a choice, I have to take this test. Regarding the consequences, I will have to leave that for now. Let's see what will happen now.

After that, the teachers gave us all the answer sheets and question papers. I saw that piece of paper, the kind of thing that everyone's afraid of whenever they see it. The thing that we call a question paper At that point, I realized I was going to completely cram.

Sorry, I don't have time to waste on talking. Only after a few seconds did I look around to see what everyone was doing. Everyone was taking this surprise test seriously. I'm also one of them. I have to write down what I have to. I wrote everything I could. My paper was completed before everyone else's, so I submitted it. But the thing is, I was the one who submitted my paper first.

I was confident that I was going to get the highest marks on this paper. So I'm going to be the topper for this exam. This paper was too easy for me. When I was about to submit my paper, suddenly everybody started to stare at me. This again. Now, what did I do? Wait a minute. Why are they looking surprised?

Sir, was taken aback as well and looked at me. It's okay for the teacher to be surprised. I can understand that. But why were these guys surprised? Wait a second, were they thinking that I'm an idiot like them? Then I'm not. I'm sorry for letting your hopes down. Now you will understand that I'm smart, not an idiot like you numb skulls.

That's it, times over. Stop writing.

Sir collected answer sheets from all of them. Now that the exam is over, I can relax.

Now that recess has started, it's time for that bastard to pay for what he did this morning. He needs to answer my questions.

So I take him to a corner to talk to him.

You bastard, why did you do that? For what reason?

(I think I know why he did that and for what reason. Since he is suspicious about me and Azuki,

Look, I don't know what you are talking about.

You know what I am talking about. I'm talking about the incident you pulled this morning.

(He must've thought that there was some kind of connection between me and Sakura.)

Incident, what incident?

I'm talking about Azuki. Why did you take her with you today?

(So he must have done that on purpose, so we can talk to each other.)

I didn't take her with me. It's just that she met me on the street. I was coming to your house just like I always do, but she saw me and called me. So that's why we were together this morning.

(Why is he calling her Azuki? Her name is Sakura, right?

(Though, to surprise you, that was my plan.)

Is that so? So why didn't you just leave me behind and go to school with Azuki?

If we were to leave you behind, I wouldn't have gotten to see the look on your face. You were so nervous. That was so funny.

(What're you talking about? I'm your friend. I consider you my friend, and you are. Because you are my friend, so I will never leave you behind.)

Hey, you are saying you didn't have what happened this morning. Don't tell me that you regret coming to school with Azuki.

If you're regretting it, then I guess I have to apologise...

We're done here. Let's meet after school.

(What an idiot. I guess I will have to change my perspective on him.)

Yeah, sure.

After school, you say? That's new and feels kind of weird coming from this guy, but it made me happy though!

Since recess had ended, we came back to the classroom. When we entered the classroom after recess, I saw Azuki was talking to someone. She was a girl. Since she is really good at talking to new people she meets, they must have become friends recently. It looked like her new friend admired her a lot. I only saw a glimpse of her eyes. She really respected Az... I mean, Sakura.

After recess ended, the teacher brought the papers and what we took in this morning. Now this is the real deal.

CHAPTER SIX

SOME PEOPLE'S ACTIONS COULD BE PAINFUL TO OTHERS.

CHAPTER 6

I was so confident that I was going to be the topper in this test. When Sir started to give us back the math papers, I was looking down on all of these numb skulls. I was full of myself that I was going to take the top spot. When the teacher started to give us back our papers, he was saying the students' names and their marks. Hearing the marks of these numb skulls makes me laugh. At last, the teacher called my name, but he didn't call my marks. I guess after seeing my marks, the teacher should be shocked that he forgot to tell everyone about my marks. Sir gave me my paper and when I saw my paper, I was also shocked at how I was able to get these marks. I rolled my paper and quietly went towards my bench. I was the class's top student, but not in a good way. This is so frustrating. I only got 5 out of

50. I was topper but from the bottom.

(Yeah, yeah, you can laugh at me now.)

After that, I didn't want to show my paper to anyone but that jerk. He took it from me. He didn't tell anyone about my marks though. That was a relief.

After that, he started to talk to Azuki. They told their marks to each other. He showed my paper to Azuki. Hey jerk, why did he tell my marks to Azuki? There was no need to do that. Azuki laughed. She laughed at me because of this jerk. He told her about my marks. Why are you doing this with me? You must be doing this on purpose. Do you hate me or something? After that, he looked at me and...

Hey Hiro, Come over here. There is something we wanted to talk to you about.

Jeez, Now what? Let's see what he is plotting now.

What do you want to talk about?

So listen, I just asked Azuki to teach you about the math paper and she said okay.

So we are going to my house. Is that okay, Azuki?

Okay, Azuki said.

Then we will go to my house after school.

Hey, what about me? Why aren't you asking me that question?

For what? Is there something you have to do after school? If you have anything to do after school, then it's a pity that you couldn't come today.

Please come with us. Hiro.

(How can I say no to Azuki?) No, there is no way I can say no to her. I guess I will have to go with them.)

Okay, I will come.

That's great.

Nope. This jerk is never going to change. He is still plotting something. When was he going to stop?

After that, Azuki left. I asked this bastard, "Why are you doing this now?"

What am I doing exactly?

[Playing like you don't know anything, huh..? I guess I don't have to argue with this guy.]

Forget it. It's nothing.

After school, I have to go to that jerk's house. What a hustle! But it's a good thing that Azuki is coming with us.

After our last class ended, she came near me and said, Hiro, I'll wait for you to at playground, so don't be late and she left. After that, that bastard came to me, so so I go with him. When I saw he looked so happy about it. He leaves early every day after school, so why does he have this much time today.

We all met at playground and I saw Azuki is standing with some girl. When I saw who is that girl was, I was surprised. But the question is why is she with Adzuki. After that Azuki introduced her. She also said that her new friend is shy and said she is also coming with us today to Kageyama's house.

I was even more surprised after hearing that. How can she come with us now.

I asked Kageyama if he not ok with it you can say no, but that bastard said " he is fine with it."

[Actually Hiro don't want her to come with them. Because he can't talk to another girl. You know how nervous he was

When he was talking to Azuki last time.]

After that she tell us her name and we also told our name to her.

When I was telling my name.....

Huh...?

She smirked at me. But why in the world she smirked at me. Is she hate me or something. But why is she hate me? We just meet each other, so there is no reason for her to hate me. She is not a shy person like Azuki told. I am really going to her if her attitude stays like that.

After that Kageyama also told her his name, but she smirked at him too. For that moment seeing Kageyama's face made me laugh.

She also hates Kageyama. I am starting to like her.

Wait a minute, I don't like her, I mean I like her but I don't like her that way. I like her because she hates Kageyama, but I don't like her that way. Ohhhh! What am I saying?! Could someone just beat me up. I don't know what am I even saying.

After that we were going together to his house. I forgot my textbook in the classroom, so I told them to wait for me, and I came into the classroom to get that book. I took that book and was about to go, but in the hallways someone stopped me. This is the guy who stares at me whenever Kageyama is with me.

There was a cold look in his eyes. The look in his eyes scares me.

Hey, there is something I wanted to talk to you about. Also, there's something I wanted to tell you before it's too late.

You know what? You really are such a terrible person, acting like you don't even care about the people who really care about you. You have to thank him that he cares about you and yet you act like he is nothing to you. How selfish can you be? It's the best feeling to have friends, and yet you act so cold with them. You have to cherish your friendship when you have a friend like him. He really is a nice person, but it really disgusts me that he is your friend. But it really disgusts me that he is your friend. It's a pity that he wants to be friends with you. He really deserves a friend better than you.

I hope you understand that.

CHAPTER SEVEN

TWO IDIOT'S MEET EACH OTHER.

CHAPTER 7

Huh..?

What the hell? What was that? What the hell just happened here and what was he talking about? He left after babbling this nonsense. How can he just leave after spouting nonsense about me?

It really made me angry after hearing what he said to me. Because of that, I really forgot everything. I really can't describe in words how much I was angry at that moment. I started to say something.

(For a moment, he becomes his old self.)

What was he talking about, again? I am selfish. A Friend? Cherish your friendship. He really deserves a friend better than me? But who the hell is he, he was talking about?

Friends, huh? I don't have any friends, you damn bastard. You have to cherish your friends, you said. How the hell am I to cherish my friends when I don't even have any? You bastard. This is easy for you to say to cherish your friendship because you are not lonely and you didn't see what loneliness looks like.

You don't even know me. What am I going through? My problems, how lonely I am, what situation I'm in, what mental torture I've been going through for years, and how I'm dealing with it all. You don't know anything about me, and yet, ohhh, right, how can you know about me? You are always surrounded by people. It feels nice to be surrounded by people, right? I also want to have friends. I really don't want to stay like this, but I am all alone. I was all alone. I will be alone. You live in light and I dwell in darkness. So there is no light for me. There was nobody there for me when I needed someone, and there will be no one there in the future either. It's a price for the sins that I committed.

Why? Why? People have problems with me. I don't get it. I just want to solve my problem. I sat on a bench. I needed to calm down. After 5 minutes, I was about to go wash my face, but for some reason, tears just came out of my eyes .

Hiro is definitely late. I wonder why he is late though.

Yeah, he is taking it for so long to just find a book.

Okay, I'll go and bring him back. Just wait for 2 minutes.

I wonder, how many minutes do we have to wait here now?

I was washing my face when suddenly Kageyama came. He asked me, "Is something happening?"

NOPE, Nothing happened, and why do you ask? Okay, let's go.

Are you sure you are okay?

I told you, didn't I, that I was okay? Look at me. I'm totally fine. Can we go now? They are waiting for us.

Sorry, guys, for making you wait so long.

Is everything alright?

Yeah, everything is fine. Don't worry.

Kageyama was suspicious of me. Somehow, he knew that I was lying earlier.

After that, we arrived at Kageyama's house. We entered his house. When we entered, I felt like something was missing in his house. The atmosphere was normal, but there was still something I felt was missing in this house. We entered his room. He brought us snacks and cold drinks. After we started to study, Azuki started to teach me the lesson that came on today's paper. When Azuki was teaching me, at that time, Hina was staring at me, and when I looked at her, she just smirked at me.

Huh..? Why was she smirking at me every time I looked at her? I guess she really hates me. Kageyama also looked at us and he looked happy. He really is a nice guy, but he irritates me by plotting schemes.

After some time, we decided to stop studying. After that, Azuki asked Kageyama something.

Kageyama, where is your mother?

He said, "She isn't living with us anymore."

That's what's missing in this house. If the mother is not at home, the house will feel empty. Fathers are always at work, working for their families, but the mother is the one who manages the house. Only the presence of the mother makes the house a happy place. He is the same as me. I know the feeling of not having someone important in your life. I really felt bad for him.

Everyone was feeling bad for him, but we couldn't do anything about it. After that, we decided to go home, so Kageyama said, "Wait a sec. I'll bring the tea for everyone. " When he left the room, the atmosphere changed. We're all feeling bad for him. He brought the tea. After that, I went home.

When I was about to leave, Kageyama said something to me. Something like 'I know that you don't consider me as your friend and you hate being surrounded by people, but one day you will consider me as your friend and the light will come to help you escape from darkness.'

Bye.

I arrived at home. I couldn't eat much that night. Today was really emotional for me and frustrating also.

Next morning,

I ate my breakfast and was about to go to school.

I'm off, mom.

Kageyama was standing in front of the house as usual, but there was something unusual today. The guy who gave me the lecture yesterday about friendship: what is he doing here? What's happening!? I was totally surprised to see him like this, but I didn't know that there was a big surprise yet to come.

After that, quietly, I asked Kageyama, "What's this guy doing with you?"

He told me about what happened yesterday at school. He said that yesterday at recce, this guy was following him and when he was alone, this guy asked him to become friends with him.

Huh..?

Then why did he lecture me about friendship? What a weird guy. When Kageyama was telling me that the guy was listening to what we were talking about, he said, "Oh, you want to know why I am here with Kageyama, right?" I'll tell you why we are together. Since you don't know how to become friends with someone else, I asked him to become friends with me. That's why we are together today. From today on, we are friends.

No, we are not friends, you stupid fool.

Ohh, that's what happened. Somehow, it reminds me of something. Ohh, how could I forget this? That's the way Kageyama started to stick with me.

(He was walking while thinking this).

When I saw back for looking at what these two idiots were doing, I discovered that they were fighting with each other. What That was a lively scene.

I tried to stop their fight, but they didn't listen to me.

He did try to tell them to stop fighting.

(He was only telling them to stop the fight in his head. He didn't say a word loudly to stop their fight.)

So instead of stopping the fight, I started to enjoy it.

Beat him up, Kageyama. Yeah, punch him with your right hand. Yeah, yeah, you are going good. Hey, new guy, what are you doing? Kick him, kick him, you idiot. I was totally enjoying their fight.

(Seeing their fight like this, he started to imagine something. Let's see what he is imagining.)

They won't have to fight like this. I won't let them fight like this with each other. I will let them fight in an official match. It's about time I had to awaken the referee within me.

You want to fight me? Tell me, tell me, that you want to beat him. Then I will give you a chance to beat him. Now those morons are in an official match and Hiro is the referee.

On my left is a young man named Kageyama, and on my right side, a young man named (I don't know) is ready to fight. Now let's begin the fight. I did a karate chop in the air and started the fight. 5 minutes later. The moment has come that we were waiting for to find the winner of this match. The winner is...

The winner of this match is Kageyama.

(That's what he was imagining.)

[He told them to stop again, but they didn't listen, so he left.]

Fight however you want, you morons.

Now Kazuma has also entered into the life of Hiro. Now let's see what will happen next.

CHAPTER EIGHT

WHO IS THE REAL ONE....??

CHAPTER 8

I reached at school but those two morons didn't come yet. I guess there were fighting for real. Anyways, let's to the classroom.

I entered in classroom. Azuki looked at me, I smiled while looking at Azuki. Hina also looked at me but she smirked at me. Why in the she smirked at me every time she saw me. After seeing that smirk look on her it ruined my mood. Up until recently she was a shy girl, right? But now I am seeing different girl who's not at all shy, that's what I think. How can she changed so quickly. I guess, I exception, though. I couldn't change myself at all.

Huh..?

Why she smirked at whenever she looked at me? I guess I know the answer she really hate me. I've surrounded by weird peoples. Later on those two morons came in classroom. Their faces were looked messed up though. Seriously, they were fighting for real. I thought they were just fighting for fun. I guess, I was wrong. That new guy is really bad news but he is perfect friend for Kageyama though. The fun is just getting started.

Now our homeroom has started. Okay it's time for studying. Let's focus on that for now. I will talk with those two morons later.

Now recess have started I can relaxed for a while. Today's teaching was hardcore. Today I bring two lunch box with me. One for me and one for that idiot Kageyama. I don't know how much time have passed since his mother is not living with them, but from looking at it, I can tell years have passed since his mother leave them. I must be hard for him. I guess, from then he hasn't eat food made by mother. Yeah, I know it might be not important thing for everyone, but I know how much important is this. Because sometimes human's can't value the things they have, we just take them as granted and can't even realize how much important that was, but they do value when they don't have that thing anymore, but it's too late for that to understand. It's just like that. I understand it, because he and I are same.

I bring the lunch for, but I don't wanna give it to him. If I give the lunch box myself then he would have thought that started to consider him as my friend and I don't want that. Even if I want, my hands are tied, so can't do that. I can't give it lunch box to him but someone else can. Okay. I have asked Azuki, because she is only one who can do this. Others two are

Okay. I'll go and asked Azuki if she can do it?

Hey Azuki, there is something I wanted asked you about. Think you can do it.

What is it?

I accidentally bought two lunch boxes with me. I accidentally bought my father's lunch with me too. Can you give one lunch box to Kageyama? But the thing is don't tell him that I bought this lunch.

Okay. I'll but on one condition.

Condition? What condition?

You don't said a word when I give this lunch box to Kageyama and we are all going to eat our lunch together. Is that okay with you.

Since I don't have choice. Okay, I'm fine with it.

Perfect. Then let's go and give this lunch box to Kageyama.

(What's going on her mind. I guess I have to see it when we get there.)

Hey Kageyama, what are doing here alone.

Nothing. Just standing around.

Okay. Take this.

What is this?

It's a lunch box. Hiro bought it for you. He said he wanted me to give it to you.

Hiro bought it? For me? That's makes me really happy, though.

(What the hell. Why she told him that I bought this lunch and for him. So that's what on her mind. Man this is so embarrassing. I guess what's done is done now, I can't do anything about it.)

Yeah. I accidentally bought it. Totally accidentally. How silly I am.

(Man this is seriously embarrassing.)

Thanks Hiro for bringing this lunch box today.

We ate our lunch together.

Food was really delicious. It's been a lone since I've ate some delicious food. Thanks again, Hiro.

It's fine. Don't mention it.

After school on my way back home I went to visit my spot, where I feel calm. I'm glad that I brought extra lunch box today for Kageyama. Doing something good, makes you to feel good, huh..? I almost forgot that feeling. He was happy though, it all that matters.

Where I am? What's really happening here? I can't see anything, I can't hear anything, I can't sense anything except this darkness.

Next day.

Good morning, Hiro

I ate my breakfast and started to go to school.

I'm off, mom.

Kageyama and the new guy were standing in front of my house as usual. I didn't say a word to them and started to walk in front of them.

Last night I had a dream. A dream that made me realized who am I really. If I put it in simple words that dream was about A pitch darkness, being swallowed by darkness, a person sitting and crying and agonized by something. That's a dream of mine. That was a scary dream, but it helped me a lot.

In that dream suddenly I was swallowed by darkness. I was unable to see anything because darkness, so I started walk to find an exit. Suddenly, I heard a voice, a voice that I know.

"where are you going, anyway." That's what I heard.

So I asked "who are you?"

It's just laughable that you had to asked that question to me.

Just tell me "who you are?"

So you really forgot about me. You really couldn't recognized me, after all.

Then suddenly, a spot of light appeared out of nowhere. Under that light there was a person sitting and crying and agonized by something.

I asked that person who are you and why are you crying?

When he heard my voice, he stopped crying and said "I am you."

What do you mean by that?

Just as I said "I am you and you are me. We both are same but at the same time we are not."

Hey, what are you talking about? I don't get it. I'm not you. Who are you anyway?

Just I thought, you really forgot about me, don't you? Just as I said earlier, "you are me and I am you." I am your inner self, Hiro. An inner self that you've abandoned left behind. You sure have changed since last time I saw you. Do your friends made you to forgot about me. It's nice huh.. to have friends and surrounded by them, to care about or someone cared about you, to help them or getting help when you are in trouble, to count on them or the feeling of someone counting on you, to trust them or getting trusted by them, to smile with them, that feeling of joy, to support, comfort, motivated by them, to do what things as your heart contents, that's what every human heart wanted. But you are not a normal human. You can't feel emotions or you don't have to.

You forgot about me, you even forgot about yourself. I don't even recognized who you really are and because of that I am suffering here alone, all by myself.

I guess, you really forgot about Azuki. The Azuki who got hurt because of your one decision, the Azuki who's suffered a lot because you, The Azuki who's lots her memories because of you, the pain and suffering you caused Azuki, you didn't even help her, You can't forgot all of it but yet here you are you forgot about everything and having with your friends.

I guess, I can't blame you, you are human too, so even you can't live all alone. That's fine. Your are feel free to do what you want. I will stay here and regret about that decision I made on that day. Goodbye, Hiro.

Suddenly I woke up. At that time I was sweating a lot. I was afraid. What he said was true. Every word he said was true.

Now what will going to happen to Hiro. We all want to know about it, right. I guess, we have to wait for next chapter to know about it. So let us meet in new chapter.

9 798887 494562

Printed by Libri Plureos GmbH in Hamburg,
Germany